1,000 Words in a Picture

A collection of short stories

Glenn Cravens

Dedicated to everyone who believed in me.

CONTENTS

INTRODUCTION

Welcome to the series "1000 Words in a Picture." The concept is to take a real-life picture and create a fictional story of exactly 1,000 words. The 1,000-word count is based off of the Scrivener word processor application. The title of the story and the picture intro page do not contribute to the word count. Each book in the series has five different fictional stories. I hope you enjoy this book, as well as future ones.

--Glenn

SUNDAY BOUQUET

Cliff kept his hopes up. A single man who just turned 30, he decided five years ago he was ready to settle in the big city and find a soul mate. Single people came to the big city to get married. Cliff, a big city lifer, remained in search.

He stuck with the same plan. Each week for the past five years, Cliff bought a bouquet of flowers as part of his grocery trip. His personal counseling business on the 10th floor of a Main Street skyscraper allowed him to live a good life. He wanted to share it with a woman, though. At the supermarket each week, he would go to the floral section and grab a bouquet of flowers, placing the lucky selection in a rusty and squeaky shopping cart. It was always the first thing he grabbed at the store. Perhaps if he bought the flowers, beautiful women at the store would see it, spark a conversation, give him their phone number and set up a date with him. Some women passed by and smiled, believing Cliff was buying the flowers for a girlfriend or wife. Others complimented Cliff on the selection outside of the store, using it as a setup to ask him for his shopping cart. The flowers never resulted in a phone number, let alone a date.

There was nothing wrong with Cliff. He took care of himself physically, wore a suit everywhere and was courteous to people. There were times when he thought he needed to stop buying flowers, only to change his mind and try to find the perfect bouquet that would get the perfect woman to say yes to a date.

It was a cold Sunday when Cliff made his latest weekly trip to the supermarket. His haul included potato chips, bread, cold cuts, apples and orange juice. But all of that came after he picked the fresh bouquet of flowers. He paid $35 for his groceries and flowers, stuffed the groceries into two reusable bags and then took the shopping cart out to the parking lot.

After opening up the back of his beat-up Jeep, he paused and looked at his Sunday haul, satisfied with the food he bought. He then stared at the bouquet of flowers. The purple lining mixed well with the yellow petals from some of the flowers. The light purple secondary flowers mixed ideally with the yellow. He couldn't understand why some flowers stayed closed. It would have made the collection brighter and more colorful than currently presented. In five years, it was one of the best bouquets Cliff had ever bought. Yet, it didn't result in a woman stopping him inside the store and talking to him. And now, he was ready to take it home to wonder.

He grabbed both of his grocery bags and slowly stuffed them into the back of his Jeep. He reached back to grab the flowers when he saw a woman right next to his cart. She looked at the flowers, then at Cliff.

"Those are beautiful. Who are they for?" the woman asked.

Cliff stuttered for a minute to catch his breath before thinking of the best words to say. Surely the woman wanted his cart. That's what all of the woman have eventually asked him the last five years.

"Thanks, they are definitely beautiful," Cliff said before shrugging his shoulders.

The woman smiled. "Yes, they are. But who are they for?"

This startled Cliff. Was this woman being nosy for no reason or serious about who the flowers were for? This was not going according to the script of the last five years, and this was awesome.

"They actually are for nobody," Cliff said as he added confidence to his tone. "They could be for you, perhaps. What is your name?"

"Melinda. And that is very thoughtful of you, but I think I'll have to pass. That is, unless you are serious that they are for nobody."

Cliff shrugged his shoulders

again, his indication that he really didn't have anyone to give the flowers to. He assured Melinda what he said earlier was correct, explaining his weekly tradition before exhaling and putting his head down in personal shame.

He looked back up at Melinda, who flashed a smile for the first time. The confident man with the smooth tone and nice suit was not his normal self in front of a woman who was wearing business attire.

Cliff grabbed the flowers and began to put them in his Jeep before pausing and presenting them to Melinda.

"Well, we've talked for this long, it might as well make sense," Cliff said.

Melinda smiled and accepted the flowers.

"I was going to get these flowers but then I saw you pick them up," Melinda responded. "Thing is, I've seen you get flowers at the store the past few Sundays, and I got curious. I didn't mean to be nosy. Always flowers, but no lady with you."

Cliff smiled. "That's just how it goes. Maybe one day."

"Maybe today is the day," Melinda

said, smiling. Clutching the flowers with her shoulder, she grabbed a pen and a slip of paper from her purse to write something. She soon put the paper in Cliff's hand and closed it herself.

"Thanks for the flowers," Melinda said softly. "Weird to do a conversation like this in a parking lot. Maybe I'll see you sometime."

Cliff looked at his closed fist and then at Melinda. "Hope so."

Melinda walked away with the flowers, tapping several yellow petals before smelling the bouquet. She got into her car nearby and drove off.

Cliff kept his fist closed, using one arm to close the back of his Jeep and then to unlock the driver's door and get inside. Cliff opened up his clenched fist to look at the crumpled paper. The ink on it was not much.

Melinda 669-221-6251 XOXO

Cliff stared forward for a few minutes.

"Maybe the flowers will work next week."

CAVE OF BATS

The three teenage hikers weren't prepared. Even with the sunshine at its brightest, they were warned by the park ranger to have a flashlight if they wanted to enter the Cave of Bats. There was a chance of bats being in there to strike any unprepared entrants. The cave lied along a shorter path to Halo Lake, but the park ranger suggested using the lengthier and bumpier Rock Trail.

K.C., Beaker and Lithi didn't listen to the park ranger, having confidence they could easily get

through the cave without a
flashlight. As they walked, the
three kids' confidence lessened in
different levels. They were 100
yards from the entrance, with
Beaker having no more faith in
getting through the cave safely.
He grabbed K.C.'s arm, and the
three stopped.

"What if there are bats?" Beaker
asked. "We're screwed if we walk
in there."

K.C. shrugged off Beaker's hand.
"We can see the other side of the
cave. We're OK. Stop worrying."

"You heard the park ranger,"
Lithi said, stuttering underneath
her breath. "We need a flashlight
for the caves. You want to get
killed by bats?"

Their open fear fueled K.C. He
planned to lie down inside the
cave's dirt floor to show his
friends he didn't fear anything.
The cave's exit was visible as
they approached the entrance to
the dark realm.

It was difficult to tell what was
in the cave, given its pitch black
tone. As the rest of the trail was
lit up by the bright sunshine, the
three wondered why more light
hadn't seeped into the cave.

K.C. asked why fear was letting

them overtake their consciousness. No response. K.C. kept walking, getting within 75 yards from the entrance.

"If there's a hole, you're going to break your ankle," Lithi said, thinking of anything that would stop K.C. That got the unabashed kid to pause for a moment. The three of them didn't know whether the cave dipped in elevation or had holes on the ground that would eat up their feet. What if all three broke their ankles on a deep hole? And how deep were the holes? One foot? Two feet? Deeper?

"That's a problem, but it's really not a big problem, because we'll be walking slow inside there," K.C. responded. "I'd be more concerned with the holes having some rats running around there biting us with their rabies. But rats mixed with bats shouldn't be a problem if we're careful."

Lithi cringed when she heard that. She remembered her biology class months ago where she was told a tale about how the feces from the bats were too much to handle for cave rats, killing them instantly. The bats would then swoop the rats in almost a ceremonial-like fashion to consume for dinner. Lithi never asked whether the story was true but it didn't matter, given she was on the brink of possibly seeing it happen.

They were within 50 yards from the cave's entrance before Lithi backed up a few steps. Beaker saw the retreat and grabbed her arm.

"No. We're all for one. We all do this, or no," Beaker said. "Let's all come to a consensus about this. What if we run?"

The cave's entrance and exit looked to be parallel, so perhaps they could run through to the other side and out. At least they could say they were in the cave.

K.C. shook his head unconvinced. He was going to walk into that cave and be consumed by its darkness for more than a few seconds.

"Running? Come on, guys," K.C. said. "You all talked about holes in the ground a second ago."

K.C. kept walking, the others slowly moving forward. They were 25 yards from the cave. Lithi's heart pounded hard. Beaker's knees shook. K.C. walked upright with confidence. As they trekked forward, the other entrance to the cave on the opposite end became brighter.

"See, guys, we can see the other end. There is nothing to worry about," K.C. said with conviction. "What y'all need to do is stop worrying about your fears and just be in awe of the amazing hike we're having right now."

Lithi ran up to K.C. and blocked his way again. As she stopped, a loud screech bellowed out of the cave.

Lithi dropped to the ground, covering her head with her arms. Beaker became a statue, his face in shock at the ear-piercing noise. K.C. turned his head in several directions.

"That's it! That's the bat, or bats, or rats, or something in there!" Lithi yelled. "Hell no! I'm not going in!"

K.C. looked at the cave's entrance, hoping to see whether something moved around inside. Maybe there were bats clinging to the ceiling. Maybe there were rodents running around on the ground and one got swooped up by a bat, or maybe something else happened.

"This should make it even more fun," K.C. said. He was as convinced as ever to go inside.

"Look, guys, I know it might not be safe, but sometimes we have to welcome danger."

Beaker and Lithi shook their heads, while K.C. looked at both of them and kept walking.

"I'm going in and you all can't stop me," K.C. said as he kept going. He was five yards from the entrance when he looked back, seeing Beaker and Lithi from a short distance.

Another screech came from the cave, louder than the previous one. K.C. hesitated. The bats were real. K.C. was ready to walk in before seeing a shadow that quickly disappeared. Fear set in. K.C. was OK with the noise but couldn't handle meeting whatever dark enemy was inside with no flashlight.

K.C. backpedaled to Beaker and Lithi. All three looked at the entrance in silence.

"You kids should have listened to me!" It was the park ranger who emerged from the cave. "I'm trying to scare the bats away because I knew you all would come here with no flashlight. It's safe in here. Follow me."

CROSSING PATHS

All right, down the home stretch. My two-mile walk is almost over. Damn it feels good to be out here this morning. It's not even eight o'clock and the sun is shining. The sky is bright and blue. The wind is crisp and light. This is a perfect morning. Thank goodness I live in a neighborhood where everyone is peaceful. This is great.

I see my house from a distance. I am, wait. What is this? No, please, no, please. A black cat is in the way. No, please. I cannot believe this black cat is in the way.

Look at this damn cat, it's in the shade of this damn tree, licking itself like it doesn't care. But I care. I definitely care.

This black cat has killed my momentum these last two weeks. Why does this stupid black cat have to be in the way when I was having a good two-mile walk?

This wouldn't matter to anyone else right now but it definitely matters to me. You see that stupid wood fence? Two weeks ago, this black cat sprinted past me while I was walking, and it startled me so badly, I tripped over the fence and broke it. Stupid bad luck, bad cat. No. I'm not moving. I'm staying right here, right in front of it. I'm not crossing its path, and if it runs at me, I'm moving backward. Running backward is probably a good thing to do. I should make it run forward so I can keep going, but I don't want to touch it. I don't even want to psych it out. I just want it gone.

Two weeks ago was when this stupid cat came into my life, I was finishing mowing my lawn when a couple of birds came down to find something to eat on the newly mowed lawn. That was fun to watch. This stupid cat then sprints on the lawn, scaring the birds, then looking at me, then sprinting away before I could catch it. That was the first salvo from him, or her, or it, or whatever this cat's gender is. I still had to finish mowing the lawn, so I pulled the lever, and I dislocated my shoulder because the lever was stuck. Damn back luck. I blame it on the cat.

Now, I'm looking at this stupid cat, and it's still not moving. It's still licking its own hair. Ugh. I could never imagine myself licking my own hair. The cat and its bad luck got the best of me back two weeks ago. And then the next day after the lawn mower incident, I go outside to wash my car, the black cat runs past me down the sidewalk. I try to be funny and spray it with some water, but he's too fast. This black cat must have had some extra tuna that day because he got away. I finished washing my car, so that wasn't a problem. But when I got back into my house, I tripped on the walkway and busted my chin open. And then I stubbed my toe five minutes later! What is this bad luck? I blame both of those incidents that day on the cat. So in less than 24 hours since that cat started tormenting me with its bad luck, I dislocated my shoulder, tripped and fell and cut my chin and stubbed a toe. What a load of crap. How can a cat possess so much bad luck?

I still haven't moved. I'm not making the first move on this damn cat. I'm ready to run back or ready to keep going forward if it moves forward. I hope it moves forward.

"Just move, you stupid idiot!"

Nope, it won't listen to me. It is still staring at me and licking its own hair.

Oh, and there was the one time where I was leaving to go to work, oh yeah, this was the worst. I got in my car and started to back up, and the cat sprinted out of nowhere. Was it under my car? Anyway, I see it leaving, it was totally scared. So I keep backing up and leave. I make a left turn to get onto 13th Street, and this truck doesn't stop. Oh my goodness, I thought I was dead, and the truck barely missed my car. Unbelievable. I could have been a dead man. That was probably the worst charm this black cat gave me. It was almost as if the black cat was trying to tell me, "How dare you take away my good shelter! Here's some more bad luck."

OK, it's time. I have to do something. I can't keep waiting. I'm backing up. Yeah, that's the strategy. This stupid cat is following me! No, please, no. Get away from me.

"Stupid cat!"

I stick my foot out, but it didn't budge. It wants to be with me. No way, man. Not going to let this happen.

I'm walking backward, keeping my eyes on the cat, and …

"NO!"

(Heavy breathing)

That minivan.

I almost got hit by a damn minivan trying to get away from this cat. Stupid bad luck getting in the way again. I blame the cat for this. No. I'm going to run now. Forget this.

= = =

(Heavy breathing)

I ran all the way around the block, and I did it backpedaling. I didn't see the cat. Well, this is good. I got that cat out of my hair, and I logged more than two miles. This might end up being a good morning after all.

How can I … ahh!

GET IT OFF ME! IT'S JUMPED ON MY HEAD! I CAN'T SEE!

= = =

All I can do is look onto the street. I couldn't see, so I threw the damn cat, and I threw it onto a speeding SUV. The cat landed on the SUV, and the SUV sped off. I just hope that's the end of the damn cat, dead or alive.

FIVE-MINUTE GAME

The tablet stood among the mess that consumed Jamal's desk. Pamphlets, manila folders and baseball lineups were mixed among press releases, clipboards and employee handbooks. It was a typical sports agent desk, except for the tablet that was showing a chess match. Jamal was a big chess fan and wanted to become a national master one day. A prime opportunity was coming soon. The city chess championship was set to start in 24 hours, the first of three steps toward a national championship and national master status.

Jamal studied chess as much as he could in between typing and negotiating. He tried to learn different strategies that could be implemented in tournament play. He's played for 10 years, but the 18-year-old kept soaking up information. He saw how opponents sneaked in a bishop H2 checkmate, or how quick opponents were to trading queens. He wanted to be ready for anything.

Jamal's strategy was to save as many pieces as possible until 'the big bomb' hit, the moment pieces were captured in a mass until either he or his opponent had almost nothing left, leaving checkmate only a couple of moves away. This strategy worked most of the time, with opponents playing the possum game alongside Jamal instead of taking his pieces at will.

Friday morning, he rested his tablet along his work computer to watch a live chess game as a means of studying for tomorrow's tournament.

As Jamal watched the game on his tablet, he received a tap on the shoulder from his fellow agent Danielle.

"What are you watching there?" Danielle asked in a nosy tone.

"It's just chess," Jamal said, laughing. "You actually know about this game?"

"Of course I do," Danielle said. "I've played a couple games here and there. I once checkmated a guy in three moves."

Jamal didn't believe her, and the two began to dare each other into playing a game. This normally would have been Danielle's smoke break, but she wanted in. This was going to be a good practice for Jamal going into tomorrow's tournament. If Danielle did dust someone in three moves, surely she could provide a decent challenge.

The two agents made an easy agreement: loser buys lunch. After a blind draw, Jamal ended up with the white pieces, Danielle with the black pieces. They set the timer for five minutes and played on Jamal's tablet.

Both agents were intent on making quick decisions. Danielle's plan was to scoop up whatever pieces she could get immediately. Jamal wanted to wait until 'the big bomb' hit, but even he got caught up in trying to take Danielle's pieces as soon as possible.

Within eight moves, neither agent had checkmate in their sights. They took pieces from each other trying to dwindle the field, but neither had a win locked up.

The scenario was frustrating for Jamal, who started to have doubts he was ready for tomorrow's big tournament. If he couldn't get past a co-worker, what would make him believe he could reach national master status?

Danielle also was frustrated. She couldn't take out Jamal in three moves, and Jamal made plays later in the match she was not ready to counter. At least she still had a chance. Her queen remained on the board even though after eight plays she had not moved it yet.

Each agent did three more moves, but no checks materialized. Jamal found an opportunity, moving his queen to A4. Danielle's king was in danger.

"Check, unless you want to resign right now," Jamal said.

Danielle gave Jamal a death stare before bringing her queen down one spot to D7. This was a big moment for Jamal. Either he could initiate a queen exchange, or he could make another move and let Danielle start the queen exchange.

"I don't think I want it," Jamal said out loud, moving his queen one spot to the left, taking one of Danielle's bishops.

Danielle didn't see a good spot to attack, so she castled. As she moved both a rook and the king to their new places, she let out a sigh realizing she could have done a different move. Jamal quickly castled.

"Open file. I'm going to take care of that," Danielle said. She took her rook on her left and moved it to E8.

Jamal calmly moved a bishop from E2 to B5. The bishop was ready to attack the queen.

Danielle picked up her queen, ready to take a pawn on D5, but she froze. The queen couldn't take the pawn, or else Jamal's knight would take the queen. Danielle's major piece was toast.

Danielle stood up and took a couple of steps back, hoping she could figure out an answer in a couple of seconds. Jamal had put enough pressure on her to leave her scrambling for an answer. The thought of playing without her queen was something she did not want to deal with.

"I'm rusty," Danielle said,

chuckling. She put her hand out, and Jamal shook it. "Good game, but I want a rematch. Guess I'll be going to the deli for both of us."

Jamal looked at the replay of the match on the tablet and was surprised he needed only 15 moves to win.

```
 1.  e4   d5
 2.  exd5 Nf6
 3.  Nf3  Nxd5
 4.  Be2  Nc6
 5.  d4   Nf6
 6.  c4   Bg4
 7.  Nc3  Bxf3
 8.  Bxf3 e6
 9.  d5   exd5
10.  cxd5 Ne5
11.  Be2  Bb4
12.  Qa4+ Qd7
13.  Qxb4 O-O-O
14.  O-O  Rhe8
15.  Bb5
```

Jamal offered to show Danielle the move sequence, but Danielle declined.

"Roast beef, no mayo, extra mustard, sourdough, two tomatoes, spinach," Jamal said. "And bring a bag of chips."

Danielle went to her desk to grab her purse and car keys. She went back to Jamal, who flashed a $20 bill.

"I just wanted the practice for tomorrow," Jamal said. "I'm ready to win. Lunch is on me. But you still have to make the drive."

TEARS IN THE CHAMBER

'The Chamber,' as Max called it for many years, was going to be emptied out. It was home to a printing press, which was the backbone for the 125-year-old newspaper company he worked for as well as the book publishing company he started as a side venture in 2007. But this was 2008, and the financial crisis hit the town worse than most. People stopped reading the daily newspaper, and the town's residents were so broke, nobody wanted to escape their daily lives by reading Max's self-published books. Sales tanked, and parts of the printing press were sold a month ago to keep the newspaper company afloat.

The Chamber used to be the place where the action happened. It was magic to see big grey rolls of paper get split into two, then the paper get splattered with ink, then the inked paper get folded into what looked like a newspaper.

Those days were long gone. The Chamber was a messy cemetery. Two blue bins, where fresh newspapers would go before being distributed, were empty sans some mice bones on the bottom. Broken crates were everywhere on the ground. Stacks of newspapers dated before 2007 sat in a corner.

The roller, where the newspapers traveled into the blue bins, was rusty and stiff. It was the last big part of the printing press that remained. Some janitors at the company challenged each other to a pull-up competition six months ago, with one injuring his back. He was soon let go by the company for his 'hijinx.'

Today, the whole company was being let go. It was bought out by its rival, which made a decision not to keep anyone. The rival thrived. It had more money and readers and a lively press. Max watched the janitor and other unruly reporters and editors get shipped out over the years for not respecting their position in the company. In three hours, he was soon to be shipped out, and he wanted to be left alone. He didn't disrespect the company. He loved the 10 years he worked for the newspaper. He was appreciative of the company allowing him to start his own publishing company, where he wrote 10 books as an indie author.

The Chamber was the place to be when the press was working. After today, machines and hired muscle would come clear The Chamber and the rest of the building out. This was why Max wanted to be here, to see it one last time. He thought he did everything right. Yet, he was not needed anymore.

He walked to the fire extinguisher that rested beyond the two blue bins and jarred it free. He shook the red can with all of his might before firing it at a bin. The extinguisher spewed foam with a fury for a half-second before dying. Max then walked to the roller and tried to do a pull-up. He might have been 350 pounds - the journalism life was not one of physical activity - but he was determined to do one pull up.

Max jumped, grabbed the red bar and strained to get his head above it. He dropped down before trying again. Nope. His arms and shoulders were toast. The janitors must have been superhuman to do 20 pull-ups, he thought.

"Man, this is another reminder to work out," Max said. "Probably my 100th reminder to work out."

Max looked around The Chamber before walking to a stack of untouched newspapers and grabbing one.

"WE TAKE BACK THE CITY" was the big headline in a November 2004 newspaper. Max remembered this fondly, having talked to the current mayor when he won the election, taking over for the previous regime that was caught playing with taxpayer money. Max uncovered a lot of City Hall drama in 2004. It was perhaps the most stressful time of Max's life, with death threats and bouts of praise coming everywhere like raindrops falling from the sky, no escape without getting emotionally touched at least a couple of times a day.

Max was a finalist for several awards in 2004 for his City Hall coverage but didn't win. Fellow reporters believed Max did so well, he was bound to win at least one award.

He was shut out.

He told himself journalism shouldn't be about awards, but even with all of the praise he received, he wondered why he didn't win at least once in 2004. He moved to the sports department three months after that election, saying it offered a new challenge.

Max clenched the newspaper and cried. Reality hit him harder than at any point in the night. There were too many emotions. He thought about what would've happened had he stayed a City Hall hound, or how his career would've changed if he won one award. He wondered what was next in his life, given he only knew newspapers and print books.

As he cried, an arm rested on his shoulder. It was Handy, his sports assistant, the kid who wanted to be sports editor in 2004 but bowed to Max because of seniority. Handy knew Max would be down here on the final day.

"I know how much you love The Chamber, but it's time," Handy said. "There's cake in the newsroom, and we're going to take a group picture."

Max looked at Handy, tears still coming down the big man's eyes. He shook his head to decline the offer.

"Nope, no way, Max," Handy said in reply, knowing Max didn't want to be in the picture. "At some point, we all have to move on. We can't live forever. Let's go."

Handy walked to the front door of The Chamber before looking back at Max, tears in his eyes. Max looked at the newspaper he held for a few more seconds before putting it back in the once untouched pile.

"Can't live forever. But damn, it sure would be nice to," Max said as he left the chamber.

JOIN THE FOLLOWING

Future editions of "1000 Words in a Picture" are in the works, and I'm very excited to bring you the next edition of the series coming September 2014. To stay updated on when the book will be released, be sure to sign up at gcravens.com/email. I'll be giving away an autographed copy of Volume 2 when it comes out.

Also check out my previous book, "Evo Moment 37."

Thanks for your support!

ABOUT THE AUTHOR

GLENN CRAVENS is an author and reporter, having been in the journalism field for almost two decades. He is actively involved in sports and video games, and he plays a lot of "Dance Dance Revolution" during the weekends. He's the author of the books "Monterey Bay Thunder," "Three in the Secret Society" and "Evo Moment 37"

You can connect with Glenn on Twitter at twitter.com/gyt. Feel free to send him email at getyourtournament@gmail.com.

PICTURE INFORMATION

Sunday bouquet
- **Device used:** Apple iPhone 4S
- **Photographer:** Glenn Cravens

Cave of bats
- **Device used:** Canon PowerShot S5 IS
- **Photographer:** Glenn Cravens

Crossing paths
- **Device used:** Apple iPhone 4S
- **Photographer:** Glenn Cravens

Five-minute game
- **Device used:** Canon PowerShot S5 IS
- **Photographer:** Glenn Cravens

Tears in the chamber
- **Device used:** Canon PowerShot S5 IS
- **Photographer:** Glenn Cravens